W9-COY-412

Psst! What you have in your hands is **TOP SECRET.** It's about Secret Agent Martha, the talking dog.

Your mission, if you choose to accept it, is to read this book. Help Martha close a case! Crack a code! Uncover the meaning behind words like *scheme* and *mastermind*!

K9 - 002

CONFIDENTIAL
TOP SECRET
CONFIDENTIAL

AGENT NAME: Martha

CODE NAME: K9-002

BODY TYPE: A dog of many parts (medium-size mutt)

PAWPRINTS:

SPECIAL SKILL: The day Martha ate alphabet soup, the letters in the soup went to her brain instead of her stomach. This mysterious event gave her the gift of Human speech. Martha claims that a bowl of Granny's Alphabet Soup every day maintains her unique skill. Although this explanation may be hard to swallow, we can confirm that Martha does speak Human . . . a lot!

METHOD OF OPERATION: Martha employs her special speaking skills to solve all sorts of crimes. One night when a burglar broke into her house, she called 911 and saved the day. On other occasions, she has corrected incomplete orders at the Burger Barn that otherwise would have left her burgerless. That would have been a crime!

FAMILY: Helen, baby Jake, Mom, Dad, and nontalking dog, Skits. (Sometimes Martha's family wishes she didn't talk *quite* so much. But who can argue with a talking dog?)

KNOWN ACCOMPLICES: Neighborhood dogs and Helen's best human friends—T.D., Alice, and Truman

ENEMIES: Most cats

RESIDENCE: Wagstaff City

OTHER: Martha enjoys hogging the sofa, controlling the TV remote, drinking toilet water, and of course TALKING! She dislikes baths and fleas.

Now that you've boned up on the facts about Martha, read her story. Dig up clues to solve the mystery. Good luck!

WGBH Copyright © 2011 WGBH Educational Foundation and Susan Meddaugh. "MARTHA" and all characters and underlying materials (including artwork) from the "MARTHA" books are trademarks of Susan Meddaugh and used under license. All other characters and underlying materials are trademarks of and copyrights of WGBH. All rights reserved. The PBS KIDS logo is a registered mark of PBS and is used with permission.

For information about permission to reproduce selections from this book, write to Permissions, Houghton Mifflin Harcourt Publishing Company, 215 Park Avenue South, New York, New York, 10003.

Library of Congress Cataloging-in-Publication Data is on file.

ISBN 978-0-547-57659-6 hc | ISBN 978-0-547-57660-2 pb

Image on pages i–iii © 2011 by Horia Varlan as "Close-up of large wood texture area" under Creative Commons license 2.0

Cover design by Rachel Newborn
Book design by Bill Smith Studio

www.hmhco.com
www.marthathetalkingdog.com

Manufactured in China
SCP 10 9 8 7 6 5 4
4500512258

MARTHA SPEAKS™

Secret Agent Dog

Adaptation by Jamie White

Based on a TV series teleplay written by Ken Scarborough

Based on the characters created by Susan Meddaugh

HOUGHTON MIFFLIN HARCOURT

Boston · New York

MARTHA, PLAIN MARTHA

Sometimes you don't need to look for adventure. Sometimes adventure finds you. That's what happened to me, Martha.

A few days ago, I was just minding my own business. Helen and I played fetch. T.D. watched us from our porch.

"Here you go," I said, dropping the stick at Helen's feet.

She threw it again. Ho-hum. Humans sure love throwing sticks. But I was bored.

"Aren't you going to fetch it?" asked Helen. "You were really excited about it a minute ago."

"Eh," I said. "I guess I've figured out how it works."

T.D. sighed. "Me, too."

"What do you want to do?" asked Helen.

"Can't we do something adventurous?" I said.

"Good idea!" said T.D.

"You have to go out and find adventure," said Helen. "You can't just expect it to come to you."

At that moment, a black car pulled up to the curb. Two people wearing dark sunglasses stepped out.

"Is one of you the talking dog?" asked the man.

I looked to my left and then to my right. No other dogs.

"Um . . . me?" I said.

"For you," said the woman, handing me an envelope.

Then they left. Just like that.

"What was that about?" I said. Or tried to say. It's hard to speak with an envelope in your mouth. Helen took it from me.

"Maybe it's an invitation to a surprise party," said T.D.

"I don't think so," I said. "I've never seen those guys before."

"Maybe that's the surprise," said T.D.

Helen opened the envelope. She read the letter aloud.

> Dear Talking Dog,
> Have you ever thought about becoming a secret agent?

"Martha? A secret agent?" T.D. said. "That would be perfect for you. You'll look like a normal dog, but you'll be fighting crime!"

"Cool," I said. "But what's a secret agent?"

"A secret agent is someone who does secret work," said T.D. "Like a spy."

A spy! I could just picture it. I'd wear a tuxedo and a tiara. Jazzy music would play wherever I went. I'd sneak into swanky places like casinos.

"I don't believe we've met," a man at my table would say.

"Martha," I'd introduce myself. "Plain Martha."

A waitress would serve me a drink. "For you. Fresh toilet water."

"Shaken, not stirred?" I'd ask. But then— *"Wait!"* I'd say, knocking the dish off the table. "I didn't order a drink."

Splash! The spilled liquid would sizzle and smoke.

"Bring me another one," I'd order. "But this time, *hold the poison.*"

T.D. interrupted my daydream. "And if the bad guys grab your collar, it could turn into handcuffs and trap them!"

"You could have a doghouse that turns into a car!" Helen added.

I was excited!

"So where do I go?" I asked.

Helen read from the letter:

131 Jones Street. Ask for the Chief.

A SOUP-ER MISSION

"This can't be right," I said. One thirty-one Jones Street didn't look like a spy agency. It looked like an auto body shop.

Clank! Bang! Clatter!

"EXCUSE ME!" I shouted to a mechanic. "I'm looking for the Chief."

He pointed toward a door in the back of the shop. I poked my head in and said, "Hellooooooooo?"

In his office, the Chief was sipping tea from behind a big desk. "Yes?"

"I'm Martha. The talking dog?"

"Ah, wonderful!" said the Chief. He stood up. "Come in. I'm glad you decided to lend us your services."

"Services?" I asked, taking a seat on the rug. "I thought you wanted me to work for you."

"Services are the jobs people, and sometimes dogs, do for other people," said the Chief. "In this job, your service will be to help us stop a terrible crime."

The Chief walked to a slide projector. He pressed a button. *Click!* A photo of a factory appeared on a screen. "I think you know this place."

"Granny's Soup Factory!" I exclaimed. Granny Flo made the alphabet soup that allowed me to speak.

"We have reason to believe that someone is trying to steal the formula for Granny's soup."

Click! Cans of soup popped up on the screen.

"The FORMULA FOR HER SOUP!" I cried. "That's horrible. *Who* would do that?"

"Well—"

"Wait!" I said. "What's a formula?"

"A formula is a recipe for something," the Chief explained. "The formula for the soup is Granny's secret list of ingredients. If another soup company stole the formula, they could put Granny out of business."

I gasped. "No more alphabet soup?"

I couldn't imagine life without speaking. How would I express my opinions? Talk on the phone? *Order pizza?*

"That's right," he said. "We need a secret agent to find out who is trying to steal the formula. And I must warn you, it might be dangerous."

Dangerous shmangerous.

"Let me at them," I said.

14

IT'S K9-002!

The Chief and I took a limo to Granny's Soup Factory. I felt almost like a real secret agent. But I was missing the best part.

"What about my disguise?" I asked. "I could wear a tux."

"You don't need a disguise," said the Chief. "You have the best disguise of all. No one will ever suspect that a dog is actually Secret Agent K9-002. That's your new code name."

I tried it out. "K9-002! Watch out, it's K9-002!" It was no tux, but I liked the sound of it.

The limo arrived at the factory and we went inside.

Granny paced her office.

"I don't know what the fuss is about," she said. "No one could steal my secret formula. It's locked up in here." She moved a portrait of Granny Elsie, the company's founder, to reveal a safe. "I'm the only one who knows the combination. Trust me. No one can get to my soup formula."

"It would be difficult," the Chief agreed. "But these spies are tricky. If they ever got your formula, you'd be ruined."

Granny thought it over. "Well, as long as I don't have to pay for the guard dogs, I suppose there's no harm."

The Chief smiled as we left Granny's office.

"What did Granny mean when she said 'dogs'?" I asked. "Is there more than just—"

GRRR!

"Yow!" I yelped. I stood wet nose to wet nose with a mean-looking mutt. "Don't do that. You could really scare someone."

He growled again. *Yum!* I thought. *Someone*
had been eating sausages.

"Martha, I'd like you to meet our other
undercover agent, K9-001," said the Chief.

RUFF!

"Of course I'm not a spy," I answered. "As if!"

"K9-001 is one of our best secret agents.
Have you seen anything out of the ordinary
today, K9-001?"

RUFF! RUFF!

"What did he say?" the Chief asked me.

"He said 'nothing out of the ordinary.' But
he thinks something will happen tonight."

"Well, K9-002, then it's up to you," said the Chief. "You're working tonight. Watch out for anything suspicious."

That night I reported for duty. The factory sure looked spooky in the dark. In the halls, I tried out my spy moves. I looked to the left. I looked to the right. I spun around.

Nothing.

I checked out the locker room. My ears stood up at the sound of a click. Somebody was unlocking the door!

The doorknob turned. A hand reached for the light switch. A shadowy figure stepped forward.

I gasped. *"YOU?"*

SOUP THIEF

"Martha?" asked T.D.

"What are you doing here?" we asked at the same time.

T.D.'s dad, O.G., stood with him, holding a toolbox.

"Hi, Martha," said O.G.

"I come here all the time with my dad. He works on the machines," said T.D. "The factory's cool at night."

"I'm sure glad it's you and not the soup thief," I said.

We followed O.G. to a machine.

"So you're doing surveillance?" T.D. whispered.

"No," I whispered. "I'm watching the factory."

"That's what *surveillance* means," said T.D. "It's when you watch really hard to see what someone is going to do or what will happen."

"Oh, surveillance!" I laughed. "I knew that. I thought you said . . . schmur . . . schmey . . . lance."

After asking permission from his dad, T.D. gave me a tour.

"I know every hiding place in this whole building," he said. "Watch this!" He pulled a book out of a bookcase. The bookcase swung out like a door. We stepped into a secret closet. Inside, a big window overlooked the factory floor.

"This is where Granny checks to see if everything is going okay," T.D. explained.

In the hall, something squeaked. *The soup thief!* I thought. T.D. and I peeked out.

"It's only the janitor," said T.D.

"We should watch him," I said. "Just to practice doing surveillance."

We watched the janitor stop in front of Granny's office. He took something out of his pocket, but it wasn't a key. He was picking the lock. Soon the door opened, and he was inside Granny's office.

The only thing that janitor wants to clean out is Granny's safe, I thought.

T.D. and I crept toward the office. We hid behind the janitor's cart and saw him looking through Granny's desk.

"What's he doing?" I whispered.

T.D. panicked. "He's coming this way!"

T.D. fled. I, uh, froze.

The janitor stuck his head into the hall. "Hello? Who's there?"

He looked right at me. YIKES! There was no talking my way out of this one. I'd have to rely on my good looks. I made my cutest face and wagged my tail.

"Ha!" laughed the janitor. "Some guard dog you are, pup."

But my tail wagged on as he walked away. *I'd found the soup thief!*

26

SOME
RUFF NEWS

"Hang on," said O.G. "What happened?"

Back where we'd left O.G., T.D. and I told him about how we'd found the soup thief.

"I've got to tell the Chief," I said excitedly.

I ran to his office and waited there all night. When he arrived in the morning, I had a lot to say. I mean, even more than usual!

"The janitor?" said the Chief. "So that's their plan. Very good work, K9-002! We'd better warn Granny."

The Chief phoned her.

"The janitor?" said Granny. "That doesn't make sense. I think your secret agent is seeing things."

"Martha is one of our best agents," said the Chief. "You'd better make sure your formula is safe."

"Well, I suppose it couldn't hurt," she said. "Hang on." Granny closed her office door and bolted it. She checked her safe while K9-001 stood guard.

After a moment, the Chief hung up.
"Granny says the formula is still safe in the, er, safe. Perhaps you fell asleep. You just dreamed that you saw the janitor."

"No!" I said. "He went into Granny's office. I wasn't the only one who saw him."

"Well, janitors *do* clean offices."

"By picking locks?" I asked. "I'm warning you, Chief. Something fishy is going on. I'm going to find out what it is!"

When I returned to the factory, I used my sniffer to do some serious snooping. I tracked the janitor to the locker room. He was on his way out. I began to follow him, when—

GRR!

Yow! It was K9-001.

"I told you not to do that!" I scolded as the janitor disappeared.

Ruff!

"You have a message for the Chief? What is it?"

Ruff!

"That makes no sense."

Ruff! Ruff!

"Oh, it's in code!"

I felt someone behind me. Slowly, I turned around. In the doorway, the janitor stared at me with his mouth wide open. UH-OH! I'd been caught red-pawed.

I fled the scene. I didn't stop running until I'd reached the Chief's office. (Do two-legged spies run this much? Where's my fancy car with the windows open and top down?) I delivered K9-001's message.

"November-29-X?" the Chief repeated.

"That's right. He said it was a code."

"It certainly is, Martha! The case is cracked.
We have all the information we need to
stop that spy." The Chief shook my paw.
"Congratulations! You saved the soup!"

Yes! I went home to share the news with Helen and T.D.

"What a story!" said Helen. "You defeated the soup thief."

"Defeat?" I said. "Isn't that what you put in your shoes?"

Helen laughed. "No, *defeat* means to beat someone at something."

"I knew there was something sneaky about that janitor," said T.D. Just then, O.G. walked by.

"Dad!" T.D. called. "Where are you going?
The factory is the other way."

"The factory is closed," said O.G.

"WHAT?" we asked.

"Someone stole the secret formula for
the soup," he said. "And they say a dog
helped them."

CRACKING
K9-002'S CODE

A dog helped someone steal Granny's secret formula? Impossible!

"That's what the other people who work at the factory said," said O.G. "Or at least, the people who *used* to work there."

"But how?" I asked. "It was locked up in the safe. No one had the combination except Granny."

O.G. sighed. "It looks like the bad guy got the combination somehow."

"We have to tell the Chief," I said.

I led them to his office. "This is it," I said when we reached the building. They didn't look so sure.

"*This* is the secret agent headquarters?" said O.G.

"Yes," I said. "Follow me."

O.G. looked around while Helen and T.D. followed me to the Chief's office. "Are you sure about this, Martha?" Helen asked.

"Yes! Come on!"

The Chief's door was open. I poked my head inside. But there was no Chief. There was no desk. There was nothing but boxes of junk!

"I'm telling you, there were carpets, drapes, and a desk," I said.

O.G. joined us. "I just talked to the manager. He says there was no spy agency here."

"But there was!" I insisted.
"I was just here this morning.
I gave the Chief the coded
message from the other dog!"

"Uh-oh," said Helen.

"Uh-oh what?" I asked.

"I hope I'm wrong," said Helen,
"but I think I know how the bad
guys got the combination."

"How?" I asked.

"*You* told them."

"I did?"

"You didn't mean to. But think
about it," said Helen. "You told
the Chief about seeing the janitor.
He had Granny check the safe. Then Granny
locked the room so no one could see her. But
she forgot about somebody."

"Huh?" I asked.

"The other dog gave you a coded message to give the Chief, right?" asked Helen.

"Holy hamburger!" I exclaimed. "K9-001 was the spy. He watched Granny put in the combination. So the coded message was actually the combination . . . November-29-X!"

But what did that mean? I put my doggy brain to work. I got nothing.

Then Helen said, "November is the *eleventh* month. X is the *twenty-fourth* letter of the alphabet. So the combination was . . ."

"11-29-24!" I said.

"And the Chief was actually . . ." O.G. began.

"The soup thief!" said the janitor. (You read that right. The janitor. He was standing in the doorway.)

"The janitor!" I cried. I leaped into a box. "HIDE!"

Actually . . ." He ripped off his uniform to reveal a dark suit. "I'm Agent Johnson." He put on sunglasses and whipped out his badge. "I've been working undercover to defeat this gang of crooks. Looks like I'm too late."

DOCTOR FELT-MARKER

"You have to admit," said O.G. as we walked home, "it was a clever scheme."

"Scheme?" I said. "You mean a sneaky plan to do something bad? That kind of scheme? The kind I fell for?"

"Don't be so hard on yourself," said Helen.

"Who would ever suspect a dog could be a spy?" said T.D.

"No one," said O.G. "That's what made it perfect. They pretended they were protecting Granny. But they had one problem. Their dog couldn't talk with the crook."

"Until I came along," I muttered. I'd wanted to be a secret agent so bad, I fell for it. Hook, line, and secret code.

At home, I moped on my chair.

"Come on, Martha," said Helen. "It's not really your fault."

"That's what you say. What if Granny doesn't make soup anymore? I won't be able to speak."

Helen turned off the light. "Don't worry, Martha. I'm sure Agent Johnson will catch those crooks."

I fell asleep. Until . . . *BRRRING!* The phone woke me late at night.

"Hello?" I answered it.

"It's Agent Johnson," said a deep voice. "We have a plan to get the formula back. But we need your help."

Agent Johnson told me his idea. The next day, I met him at a lab.

"Glad you could make it," said Agent Johnson. He introduced me to the Professor, the head of their operations.

"Pleased to meet you," said the Professor. He showed me a photo of the Chief and K9-001. "Are these the culprits?"

"Yes!" I said.

"Just as I thought," said the Professor. "The man you're looking for is a criminal mastermind. You know, a person who plans a complicated crime? His name is . . . *Doctor Feltmarker.*"

"He has a secret hideout," added Agent Johnson. "No one has ever been able to find it."

"Here is a very rare picture of it," said the Professor.

"The *sky?*" I asked, looking at a photo of clouds.

"It's not just the sky. In the middle of the picture is his hideout," he said. "It's an invisible dirigible."

"An invisible dirigible?"

Agent Johnson nodded. "An invisible dirigible."

"An invisible dirigible. Very clever," I agreed. "Only . . . what's a dirigible?"

"It's a kind of giant balloon people fly around in," said the Professor. "But Feltmarker's dirigible is invisible. Here's what we think it looks like."

That's where I came in, they said. Dogs have an excellent sense of smell. I might not be able to see an invisible dirigible. But I could smell it.

"I'm happy to be of service," I said. "Just one question. That guy knows what I look like. Shouldn't I have a disguise?"

"Hmm. Not a bad idea," said the Professor.

I crossed my paws for a tux. But a moment later, I was wearing something VERY different.

"Not exactly the disguise I had in mind," I said. *Grr.*

"Well, very few dogs have a diamond collar," said the Professor.

IN THE INVISIBLE DIRIGIBLE

In his dirigible, the "Chief" put on his disguise. He drew a mustache on his face to become . . . the evil *Doctor Feltmarker!*

Feltmarker held up the soup formula. "My plan worked perfectly!" he laughed.

He had not only stolen Granny's formula. He'd nabbed Granny, too! Nearby, she sat trapped in a chair. K9-001, otherwise known as Bruno, stood watch.

"The soup formula is ours! NOW WE'LL CONTROL THE WORLD!" Feltmarker cried. "Or, er, at least the soup world."

WOO! WOO! WOO! An alarm rang.

"What's that? Is something
following us?" Feltmarker asked.
He looked at a radar screen. A small
dot blinked. "Too small to be a plane."
He shrugged. "Bah, it's nothing!"

But it wasn't nothing. It was a flying pink
poodle. Yes, it was yours truly. The Professor
had strapped a flying pack to my back. Flying
through the sky, I followed my nose to
Feltmarker's hideout.

Sniff! "That's engine exhaust, all right," I
said. "And it's coming from that dir—" *BONK!*
My nose bounced off something hard. "Ha!
Found it!"

Hovering over the hideout, I hit a switch
on my pack strap. A gush of paint spurted out.
Within seconds, the dirigible was no longer
invisible. It was orange.

"Made it," I said, landing on the roof. "Flying pack off!"

The pack landed behind me. I slipped through the roof's small door. Inside, lights flashed.

"TRESPASSER ALERT! TRESPASSER ALERT!" said a robotic voice.

"Trespasser?" said Feltmarker.

"A trespasser is someone who has gotten inside who isn't allowed," said the computer.

"I know what a trespasser is!" he snapped. "Who's trespassing in my dirigible?"

The computer's screen displayed me in disguise.

"A poodle? We'll see about that."

Feltmarker and Bruno hurried out of the control room to find me. Taking over the soup world would have to wait.

"Where are you?" Feltmarker called.

"Aha!" He bent down to inspect a trail of orange pawprints. "Whoever you are, you're smart enough to dump paint but not smart enough to keep from stepping in it!"

Feltmarker followed the tracks to a pink tail sticking out from around a corner. He grabbed for it.

"Got you!" he snarled.

HAPPY ITCHING!

Feltmarker held something up by the tail.
A pink poodle . . . *costume*. (Pretty sneaky
of me, eh?)

"A disguise?" he said.

While Feltmarker
puzzled over the
missing poodle,
I freed Granny.

"You saved me!"
she cried.

"No time for thanks," I said. "There's a
flying pack on top of the dirigible. Go for it!"

Granny ran for the door. At the last
moment, she turned back. "What about you?"

"I'll keep them busy while you escape. Hurry!"

As Granny raced off, I found the formula
and ate it. Blech. Not as tasty as the soup. I
gulped down the last of it just as Feltmarker
and Bruno burst in.

"Where is she?" Feltmarker said to himself. "Where's Granny Flo?"

"Long gone, Feltmarker," I said, stepping out from behind a chair.

"So it's you! I should have known."

"That's right. I'm sorry to inform you that your little scheme didn't work. You're defeated."

"Oh I am, am I?" Feltmarker took a bone out of his pocket and threw it at me. "Fetch, doggy!"

"Sorry, Feltmarker. But I'm in no mood for—" *Hiss.* Green mist rose from the bone and filled the air. "Sleeping . . . gas . . . zzz."

When I awoke minutes later, I found myself trapped in some kind of glass bubble.

"Where am I?" I murmured.

"Don't you know?" said Feltmarker. "You're in the *big time* now. Ha!"

It was true. I was in a huge hourglass. Feltmarker cranked its handle. The hourglass tipped.

Oof!—I fell to the bottom. Tiny black dots rained down on me.

"So you think you can bury me in sand, eh, Feltmarker?"

He cackled. "Oh, no. That isn't sand."

The sand hopped. It itched. It was . . .
"FLEAS!" I cried.

"I'll be leaving you to have a good time with your friends," he said. "But don't worry. It won't be long."

Feltmarker turned to his control panel. "Computer, set for self-destruct!"

"Are you sure you want to self-destruct?" the computer asked. "Nothing will be saved. Press yes or cancel."

Feltmarker pressed a button. "Er, yes."

"*Self-destruct* means that something destroys itself, so that nothing is left. You *do* know that, don't you?" said the computer.

"Yes, yes."

"Self-destruct. Everything blows up. KERPOW!"

"Yes, yes, *YES!*"

"All right," said the computer. "Self-destruct in two minutes. Don't say I didn't warn you!"

"You'll never get away with it, Feltmarker!" I cried.

"I'm sorry," he said, strapping on a parachute vest. "I'd love to stay and chat, but I'm a little pressed for time."

Feltmarker and Bruno jumped out of the dirigible. "Happy itching!" he shouted.

Meanwhile, the computer counted down. 1:52 . . . 1:51 . . . 1:50 . . .

It looked hopeless. *Was there no fleeing Feltmarker's fleas?*

KERPOW!

Invisible dirigible. Say that three times fast.
It's almost as impossible as escaping from one
while trapped in an hourglass full of fleas.

The clock ticked on. 1:21 . . . 1:20 . . . 1:19 . . .

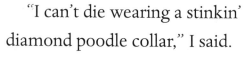

"I can't die wearing a stinkin'
diamond poodle collar," I said.

Wait a minute, I thought.
*Diamonds! It's a good thing Agent
Johnson and the Professor didn't
skimp on my disguise.*

1:05 . . . 1:04 . . . 1:03 . . .

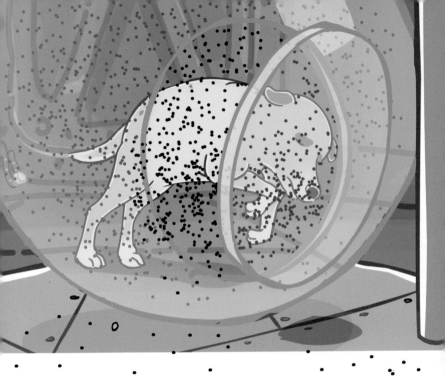

I yanked off the collar. Holding it with my teeth, I used the diamond to cut a circle in the glass. Then I pushed, and the glass fell out. (My coolest spy move yet!)

00:59 . . . 00:58 . . .

Oh, no. OH, NO. The place was seconds away from going KABOOM! I looked at the computer's buttons. One of them *had* to stop it!

If only I weren't so itchy. Argh! I scratched
and scratched. My paw accidentally hit a
button. Everything started blinking red.
Somehow I had a feeling that wasn't good.

"Ten seconds to self-destruct," said the
computer.

Yow! What do I do? What do I do? I ran back
and forth. "Pull yourself together, Martha," I
told myself. "After all, you are a secret agent."

"Five seconds," said the computer.

YOW! WHAT DO I DO? WHAT DO I DO?

"Martha!" a voice called.

Just outside the open door, Granny hovered in the air. She was wearing my flying pack.

"Jump!" she cried, holding out her arms.

I leaped, and we escaped, just as . . .
KERPOW! The dirigible exploded behind us.

"Whoa! That was close," I said.

"Look down below!" said Granny.

We floated toward the Come-On-Inn. I
could already smell their sausages. *Mmm.* I
love the smell of sausages.

"HELP! HELP! GET US DOWN!"
someone shouted. Dangling from a tree were
Feltmarker and Bruno. Granny and I flew over
to them.

"It looks like you two decided the Come-On-Inn is a nice place to hang out," I said.

Feltmarker looked surprised. Then he looked . . . itchy. Lots of tiny black dots were falling onto his head.

"What is that?" he asked. "Rain?"

"No." I smiled. "Fleas."

"FLEAS? NO! GET ME OUT OF HERE!" hollered Feltmarker. "HELP!"

Granny and I landed as the bad guys scratched like crazy.

"You did it, Martha!" said Agent Johnson, suddenly appearing. "You saved the soup!"

Only . . . I didn't.

SAUSAGE BREATH

"Martha? Wake up," said Helen. "You're talking in your sleep."

I opened my eyes. "You mean I was just dreaming? I haven't really caught those crooks?"

"Sorry," said Helen.

Grr. I hate it when it all turns out to be a dream. As Helen made me soup, I told her all about it. "It made me hungry for sausages."

"Well, all we have is soup. And not much more of it if they don't catch those bad guys," said Helen.

"The funny thing is, I feel like I've smelled those Come-On-Inn sausages somewhere else recently. But where?"

Then it hit me like bad dog breath. "Sizzling sausages! I remember."

I raced out the door to get Agent Johnson. He followed me, and I followed my nose— straight to the Come-On-Inn.

We found the crooks just where I thought they'd be. At a table, they were gobbling up the best sausages in town. They sure looked shocked to see me again.

"It's over, Feltmarker—er, Chief!" I said.

And that's how we snagged the soup thieves. Granny's alphabet soup was SAVED!

"Great work, Martha," said Agent Johnson. "But how did you figure out where those crooks were hiding?"

"Simple. By using my sense of smell. I'd smelled sausages my first day on the job. It was the Chief's dog's breath. There's only one place in town that serves sausages with that delicious, tender, tasty . . ."

"I get it," said Agent Johnson.

"Sorry. With that nice sausage smell," I said. "But it wasn't until I had my dream that I remembered where those sausages came from. The Come-On-Inn! Then I knew this must be where those crooks were hiding."

"Your dream saved the soup recipe," said Agent Johnson. "I don't know how we can ever repay you."

"Well, I have a thought." I licked my lips.

Agent Johnson laughed. "Okay, Martha. The sausages are on me."

So there you have it. Thanks to my superduper sniffer, Granny's soup was back on the burner. Mission accomplished!

But bad guys, beware. You have not seen the last of . . . Martha. Plain Martha.

GLOSSARY

H ow many words do you remember from the story?

defeat: to beat someone at something, to win

formula: a recipe for something

mastermind: someone who plans a complicated project or activity

secret agent: someone who does secret work

self-destruct: to destroy oneself or itself

service: a job someone does for others

scheme: a sneaky plan, usually to do something bad

surveillance: to watch carefully to see what someone is going to do or what will happen

trespasser: someone who has entered a place without the owner's permission

Send a
Secret Message

To write secret messages to your friends, use K9-001's code or make up your own. You can create an invisible letter by using a white crayon on white paper. Make your message appear by coloring over it with a marker.

K9-001's Secret Code

1	2	3	4	5
A	B	C	D	E

6	7	8	9	10
F	G	H	I	J

11	12	13	14	15
K	L	M	N	O

16	17	18	19	20
P	Q	R	S	T

21	22	23	24	25
U	V	W	X	Y

26
Z

Psst. Do you want to be a secret agent like me? Then take my super spy test. To pass, crack the code of eight or more of the sentences below. (Hint: use K9-001's code from the story.)

1. To become a 13 - 1 - 19 - 20 - 5 - 18 - 13 - 9 - 14 - 4 , plan a big crime and perfect an evil laugh. Muwhahaha!

2. A cat in a dog park is a 20 - 18 - 5 - 19 - 16 - 1 - 19 - 19 - 5 - 18 .

3. My 6 - 15 - 18 - 13 - 21 - 12 - 1 for the perfect snack = sausage + sausage + sausage!

4. Feltmarker's 19 - 3 - 8 - 5 - 13 - 5 to steal the soup formula landed him in hot water.

5. My 19 - 5 - 18 - 22 - 9 - 3 - 5 - 19 include sniffing out lost shoes and garbage. Mmm!

6. No one can 4 - 5 - 6 - 5 - 1 - 20 Skits at catching flying objects.

7. When I did 19 - 21 - 18 - 22 - 5 - 9 - 12 - 12 - 1 - 14 - 3 - 5 in Granny's factory, I was *soup-rised* to see T.D.

8. If you pass this test, your code name —is

   19 - 5 - 3 - 18 - 5 - 20   1 - 7 - 5 - 14 - 20 – 003!

9. Warning: this page will 19 - 5 - 12 - 6 – 4 - 5 - 19 - 20 - 18 - 21 - 3 - 20 in five seconds. (Just kidding!)

Answers:
1. mastermind, 2. trespasser, 3. formula, 4. scheme,
5. services, 6. defeat, 7. surveillance, 8. Secret Agent, 9. self-destruct

Master of
Disguise

A good spy blends into any surrounding. To create your own disguise, mix and match clothing and props. Try sunglasses, hats, scarves, uniforms, and long coats. Change your hairstyle. Use makeup to draw a mustache, wrinkles, or a black eye. No one will ever guess your true identity!